Blue Dot Kids Press

www.BlueDotKidsPress.com

Original North American edition published in 2021 by Blue Dot Kids Press, PO Box 2344, San Francisco, CA 94126. Blue Dot Kids Press is a trademark of Blue Dot Publications LLC.

Original North American edition edited by Summer Dawn Laurie and designed by Teresa Bonaddio

Original Australian edition designed by John Canty

Original Australian edition first published in 2019 by Magabala Books Aboriginal Corporation, 1 Bagot Rd, Broome (PO Box 668 Broome 6725), Western Australia, www.magabala.com, sales@magabala.com

This North American edition is published under exclusive license with Magabala Books Aboriginal Corporation.

BLUE DOT KIDS PRESS

Cataloging in Publication Data is available from the United States Library of Congress.

ISBN: 9781736226469

FSC
www.fsc.org
MIX
Paper from responsible sources
FSC™ C136333

The illustrations in the book are created using acrylic paint (red and yellow ochre, white and black) on 100 percent rag paper.

Printed in China with soy inks.

First Printing

Sally Morgan   Johnny Warrkatja Malibirr

Little
Bird's
Day

BLUE DOT KIDS PRESS

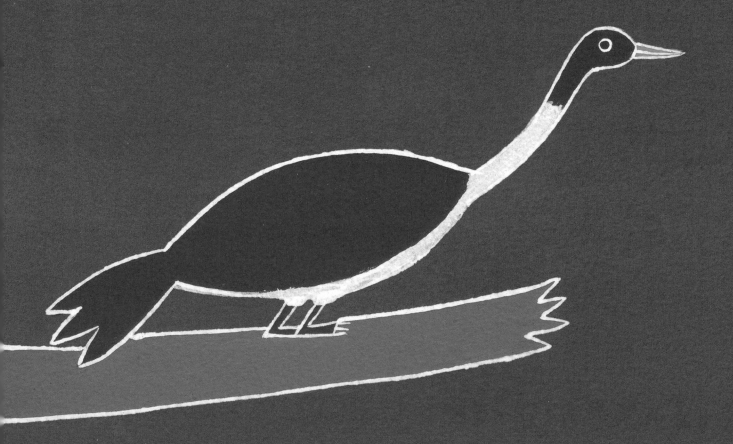

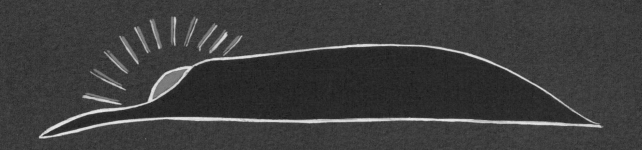

Here comes Sun,
rising and shining.

Time to stretch, Little Bird,
time to sing the world alive.

I warble with Sun
to wake the lazy sleepers.

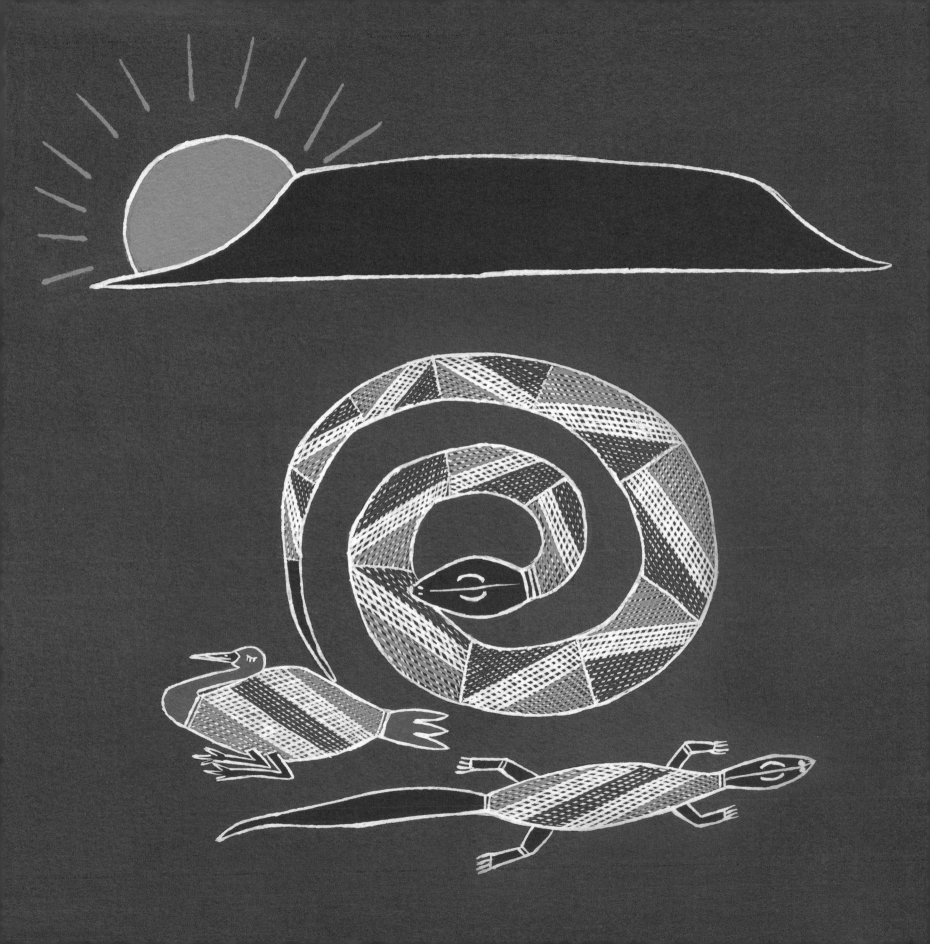

Here comes Wind, blowing and gusting.

Time to eat, Little Bird,
time to feast in the flowers.

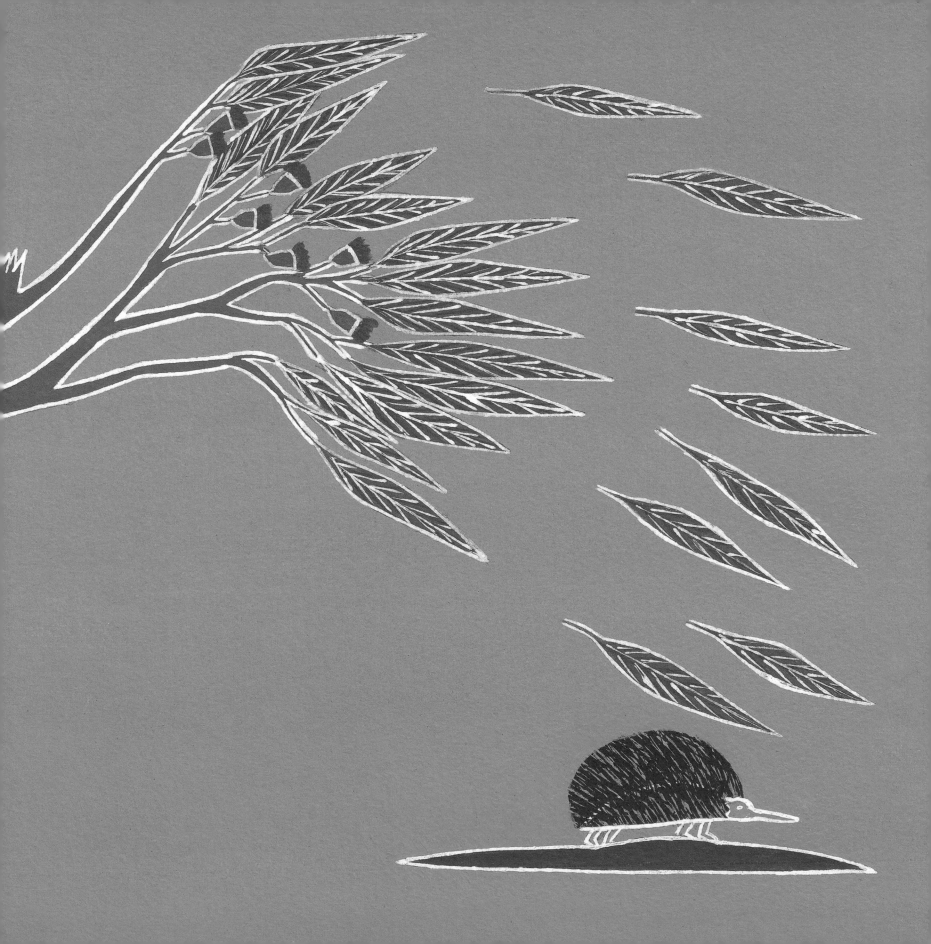

I soar with Wind
to reach the crimson blossoms.

Here comes Cloud, huffing and puffing.

Time to play, Little Bird,
time to spin across the sky.

I glide with Cloud
to chase my feathery friends.

Here comes Rain,
falling and splashing.

*Time to bathe, Little Bird,
time to sparkle with freshness.*

I flutter with Rain to wash my fuzzy feathers.

Here comes Dusk,
gliding and sighing.

Time to fly, Little Bird,
time to join a nightfall roost.

I journey with Dusk
to find a welcoming tree.

Here comes Moon,
glowing and whispering.

Time to rest, Little Bird,
time to settle with your family.

I nestle with Moon
and dream I'm flying among the stars.

*I*ndigenous peoples have been living on the Australian continent for millennia (that's thousands of years!). Indigenous Australia is made up of Aboriginal Australians and Torres Strait Islanders from hundreds of different and distinct nation groups, each with their own culture, customs, language, and laws. These clan groups are the oldest living cultures in the world.

Author Sally Morgan belongs to the Palyku people from the eastern Pilbara region of Western Australia. Sally is one of Australia's best-known Aboriginal writers. Illustrator Johnny Warrkatja Malibirr is a Yolŋu man from the Ganalbingu clan in Arnhem Land in the Northern Territory of Australia. His paintings depict Ganalbingu songlines as well as his mother's Wägilak clan stories. *Little Bird's Day* is his debut as an illustrator. As the winner of the Kestin Indigenous Illustrator Award in 2017, Johnny was invited to illustrate a manuscript by Sally Morgan. Together, the story and illustrations create a distinctly Indigenous book with universal appeal.

Johnny's illustrations reflect the distinct style of Yolŋu artwork. The color palette is based on the natural pigments of red, yellow, black, and white, and the animals are embellished with cross-hatching, a traditional raark design. To see how Johnny creates his art, check out the videos at https://gapuwiyak.com.au.

Little Bird is a silver-crowned friarbird, or Djulwaḏak. "In their songlines," Johnny says about his mother's clan, "there is a song that tells about Djulwaḏak at Warrarra [sunset], calling out to the Yolŋu to come to the ceremony ground called Bumbula. Djulwaḏak calls to everyone in their own language. Still today the Djulwaḏak sounds like he is calling out in different languages. Yolŋu can't believe how clever he is."

Many of the animals Little Bird meets are local to the
Arnhem Land region where the illustrator is from.

Can you find them all?

water buffalo   snake   lizard   brolga (crane)

frilled-neck   dingo (dog)   kangaroo   echidna
lizard   (spiny anteater)

long-necked   freshwater
turtle   prawn

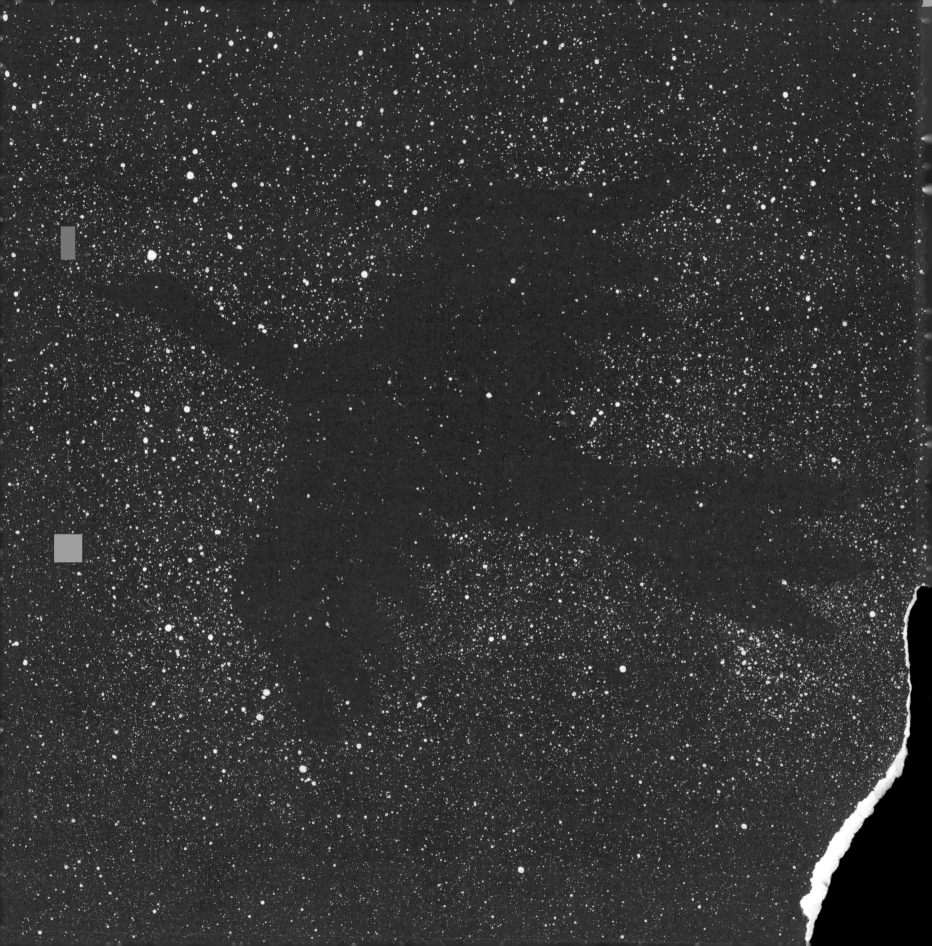